For Wesley and Clara, who share their colors with me every day
J. Y.

For Natalie and Ayden
C. C.

Text copyright © 2013 by Jessica Young
Illustrations copyright © 2013 by Catia Chien

First edition 2013

Library of Congress Catalog Card Number 2012950616
ISBN 978-0-7636-5125-1

13 14 15 16 17 18 TLF 10 9 8 7 6 5 4 3 2

Printed in Dongguan, Guangdong, China

This book was typeset in Badger.
The illustrations were done in acrylic.

Candlewick Press
99 Dover Street
Somerville, Massachusetts 02144

visit us at www.candlewick.com

My Blue Is Happy

JESSICA YOUNG

illustrated by CATIA CHIEN

CANDLEWICK PRESS

My sister says that blue is sad
Like a lonely song.

But my blue is happy

Like my favorite jeans

And a splash in the pool on a hot day.

"Yellow is cheery," says my mom.

"Like the summer sun."

But my yellow is worried

Like a wilting flower

And a butterfly caught in a net.

The boy next door says red is angry
Like a dragon's burning breath.

But my red is as brave as a fire truck
And my superhero cape.

"Pink's my favorite," my best friend says.
"It's pretty, like a ballerina's tutu."

But my pink is annoying
Like an itchy bug bite

And gum that gets
stuck to my shoe.

Dad says brown is ordinary
Like a plain paper bag.

But my brown is special
Like chocolate syrup . . .

And a piece of earth
that's just for me.

"Look," says Grandpa. "Green is young.

Like a small stem stretching toward the light."

But my green is as old as a forest

And the statue in the park.

My cousin says that orange is fun
Like a bouncing basketball.

But my orange is serious
Like a warning sign
And a tiger on the prowl.

"Brrr!" Grandma says. "Gray is cold.
Like the sky before a storm."

But my gray is as cozy as a curled-up kitten

And the sound of soft rain on the roof.

"*Shhhh . . .*" says my brother.
"Black is scary.
Like shadows c-r-e-e-p-i-n-g
across the wall."

But my black is peaceful

    Like the still surface of a lake

    And the spaces between the stars.

I guess colors are how you see them. . . .

And my blue is happy.